SPACE SCOUT ™

SCOUTING THE UNIVERSE FOR A NEW EARTH

The Dark World
published in 2011 by
Hardie Grant Egmont
85 High Street
Prahran, Victoria 3181, Australia
www.hardiegrantegmont.com.au

A CiP record for this title is available from the National Library of Australia

Text copyright © 2011 H. Badger
Illustration and design copyright © 2011 Hardie Grant Egmont

Cover illustration by D. Mackie
Illustrated by D. Greulich
Series design by S. Swingler
Typeset by Ektavo
Printed in Australia by McPherson's Printing Group

1 3 5 7 9 10 8 6 4 2

THE DARK WORLD

BY **H. BADGER**

ILLUSTRATED BY **D. GREULICH**

hardie grant EGMONT

CHAPTER 1

'How's your ice-cream sundae, Jett?' asked Kip Kirby. 'Hot enough for you?'

Kip and his best friend Jett were spending a rainy Saturday at the One Moon Shopping Mall.

It was freezing, so Kip and Jett had headed straight to the ice-cream shop to warm up. In the year 2354, ice-creams were served steaming hot. Cold ice-cream was *so* last millennium.

Kip licked his toasty caramel ice-cream. He practically never got to hang out having fun like this.

Normally, Kip was busy with school or with his job as a Space Scout.

The Space Scouts explored unknown galaxies for a second Earth. The current Earth was so crowded with people that it would soon run out of room. The future of all humans was riding on Kip and the 49 other Space Scouts.

Some people would have crumbled under the pressure. After all, Kip was only 12 years old. The other Scouts were older

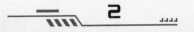

and more experienced. But although his job came with huge responsibilities, Kip absolutely loved it.

He'd seen some awesome planets on his missions — some freaky, some scary, some fun. He never knew what was waiting for him when he blasted into space. That was the coolest part of the job.

'Want to check out the pet shop?' Jett asked, leaning forward. A motion-sensitive moist serviette on a mechanical arm popped out from the middle of their table. It wiped Jett's sticky mouth then disappeared again.

Jett *loved* the pet shop. Every time they came to the mall, Jett spent ages staring

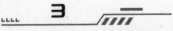

in the window. He had serious allergies to animals and wasn't allowed his own pet.

Before leaving the ice-cream shop, Kip and Jett bought a packet of Flamin' Asteroid Chips to eat on the way. They simply swiped plastic cards, and the chips popped up through a hole in the shop counter. All the shops at the One Moon Mall were completely automatic, with no-one serving in them.

The mall was 50 storeys tall and hundreds of square kilometres wide. There were 803 sportswear shops, 667 burger bars and 1407 different sneaker stores. Walking to the pet shop would take ages!

'Let's take Locata Arms,' Kip suggested.

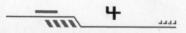

The mall was shaped like a colossal doughnut. Suspended from the roof in the very centre was a huge bunch of Locata Arms. These were mechanical arms with claw-like grippers on the end.

Kip walked up to the nearest free arm. As soon as the arm's computer detected him, the claw closed firmly around his chest.

'Pet Palace, 30th floor, east wing,' Kip said clearly.

There was a whirring of gears, and Kip's feet were lifted off the ground. The Locata Arm carried him straight to the door of Pet Palace. Jett followed in another Locata Arm.

Twelve-legged
Dodecon Spider

Glow-in-the-dark
Florg

Micro-rhino

Greater Avanian
Toucan

Gallumping Neenob

RoboPup

The Pet Palace windows were filled with alien pets like glow-in-the-dark Florgs, which were bird-beaked snakes that came from the distant Ur galaxy.

The shop was having a sale on micro-rhinos. These mouse-sized rhinos were native to a planet called Bron, and could be trained to ride on your shoulder. Jett wanted one more than anything.

Kip watched as Jett pressed his nose against the glass. Luckily for Jett, the pet shop window was specially sealed. Nothing that could trigger allergies could escape.

'Should I go in and hold a micro-rhino?' Jett said. 'Maybe my allergy has cured itself.'

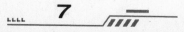

'Don't risk it,' Kip replied. Jett's animal allergy was so bad that if he even *sniffed* an animal, his skin turned blue, his eyes bulged and his fingernails fell out.

Kip was about to remind Jett of this when he felt his SpaceCuff buzzing.

SpaceCuffs were the powerful mini super computers that all Space Scouts wore on their wrists. Kip checked his screen.

**MESSAGE FROM:
WORLDCORP MISSION CONTROL**

A wormhole to a promising planet called Neron has opened up unexpectedly. Go immediately to the Intergalactic Hoverport to begin your next mission.

Incoming message

Kip felt a bubble of excitement in his stomach. He couldn't *wait* to get back into space!

Then he remembered. He'd been planning to go to the Virtual Sports Centre to practise virtu-surfing that afternoon. His mum was coming to pick him up in ten minutes.

Kip loved virtu-surfing. But with the future of Earth at stake, there was no way he could go.

The real question was, how could he get to the Hoverport quickly?

Kip thought hard, but he knew there was only one answer. He'd have to ask his mum to drop him at the Hoverport.

Kip kept a spare spacesuit, helmet and gear in the back of his mum's SnapDragon for this kind of emergency.

Bet no Space Scout's ever turned up for a mission with his mum, though, he thought, cringing.

That was about the most uncool thing in the known universe!

CHAPTER 2

The airspace above the mall buzzed with spacecraft. The massive parking area was jam-packed.

Kip checked the time on his SpaceCuff. 5.30pm! His mum would be here to pick him up any second. Jett had already gone home with his mum.

Kip scanned the sky for his mum's

SnapDragon. Almost every family had one of these buzzing personal short-flight spacecraft. Kip's mum's was bright blue with a yellow sign on the side:

SPACE SCOUT ON BOARD

There it was, streaking towards him.

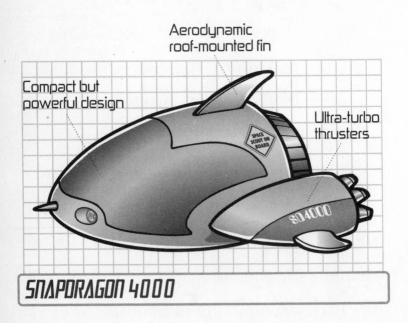

Aerodynamic roof-mounted fin

Compact but powerful design

Ultra-turbo thrusters

SD4000

SNAPDRAGON 4000

'Hurry,' Kip's mum called as the SnapDragon touched down. 'I'm almost late for Venusian Folk Choir practice.'

Kip felt bad as he jumped in next to her. His mum loved Venusian Folk Choir. But he really needed a lift!

He paused for a moment, thinking about how he should ask his favour.

'You look nice today, Mum,' he began.

'Do I? Thanks…' his mum smiled before trailing off. 'Kip Kirby, are you about to ask a favour?' she asked, laughing.

She saw right through me! Kip thought.

'Could you please give me a lift to the Hoverport?' he pleaded. 'I just got a message about an urgent mission.'

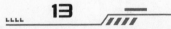

Kip watched guiltily as his mum entered the Hoverport's co-ordinates into the trip computer. She'd miss choir. But he knew she understood that he was missing virtu-surfing too. With the future of Earth's people at stake, there was nothing else for it.

The Hoverport was inside Earth's atmosphere, about 10 kilometres off the ground. All intergalactic space flights departed from there, so it was very busy. Kip's starship, MoNa 4000, was docked there when Kip wasn't on missions.

Kip soon spotted MoNa's pointed nose cone and gleaming black thrusters.

'If you drop me here, I'll spacewalk the

rest of the way,' Kip suggested to his mum.

He wanted to avoid the embarrassment of turning up for a mission with his mum! But Mrs Kirby insisted on taking Kip to MoNa's landing bay door.

Kip groaned. MoNa would never let him live this down! Teasing Kip was her favourite thing in the galaxy.

MoNa's door slid open. With his helmet and spacesuit on, Kip leapt the short distance from the SnapDragon to the landing bay. When he boarded, MoNa's laughter was echoing all around.

'Don't worry about her,' said a friendly, growly voice. 'Space Scouts do whatever it takes to get the job done.' It was Finbar,

Kip's second-in-command.

Finbar was tall and covered with white fur. He was half-human, half-arctic wolf, but his personality was more like a teddy bear's.

Together, Kip and Finbar headed for the Bridge, MoNa's command centre. There, Kip could pilot MoNa using the holographic console as well as download his mission brief.

While Kip prepared, MoNa would fly herself out of the Hoverport and into deep space on auto-pilot.

Kip settled into his captain's chair, engaged his holographic console and began to read.

SPACE SCOUT
KIP KIRBY
MISSION BRIEF

WorldCorp's sources have heard rumours that the distant planet of Neron is a wealthy trading port.

The local aliens are probably smart businesspeople. They may be willing to share their planet with Earthlings in need – for a price. Before WorldCorp can suggest this, you must explore Neron and decide if conditions are suitable for humans.

WorldCorp's astronomers say the wormhole will open at exactly 6.34pm, Earth time.

CLASSIFIED

6.34pm? That's only a few seconds away! thought Kip.

Through MoNa's massive windows, Kip and Finbar scanned the sky for the wormhole.

Wormholes were shortcuts between galaxies. Usually they glowed with light shining through from the galaxy beyond.

But this time, the only thing visible in the night sky was a faint, murky black patch of cloud.

If that's the wormhole, Kip thought uncertainly, *it must be super dark on Neron. There's no light shining through.*

Pushing a button on his console, Kip switched off MoNa's auto-pilot and took

the controls. Flying through a wormhole took Kip's advanced skills. Especially when the wormhole was pitch-black!

With a deep breath, Kip flew MoNa into the wormhole. The entire Bridge was plunged into darkness.

CHAPTER 3

Kip was in luck. The wormhole might have been dark, but at least it was calm and easy to fly through. MoNa popped out the wormhole into Neron's galaxy completely unharmed.

Neron's galaxy was so dark that Kip could hardly see a thing. Up ahead, though, he made out a dull, black ball of a planet.

Kip and Finbar strode to MoNa's landing bay. It was time to travel to Neron via Scrambler Beam. Scramblers separated their particles, beamed them through space and rearranged them on the surface of Neron.

When they arrived on the surface, Kip heard an eerie moan.

'Finbar?' he whispered. Finbar hated travelling by Scrambler!

But the moaning was the wind, whipping wildly around them. Kip analysed the air. According to his SpaceCuff, it was safe to breathe…but freezing!

Kip and Finbar carried limited oxygen. To save supplies, it was always best to

breathe a planet's own air if possible. Kip took a deep breath, not looking forward to taking off his helmet. He made sure his HeatCheeks balaclava was switched on.

HeatCheeks had heating elements woven through the fibres. When switched on, they glowed as red as a hotplate.

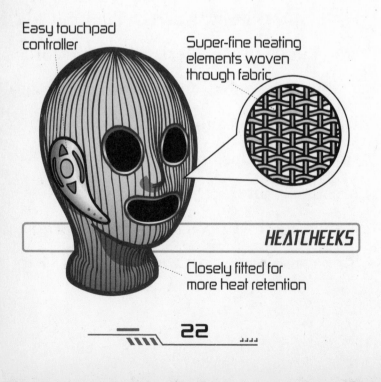

Easy touchpad controller

Super-fine heating elements woven through fabric

HEATCHEEKS

Closely fitted for more heat retention

They allowed Kip and Finbar to go without helmets in freezing conditions.

Finbar was especially keen to protect his new WhiskerMic from the cold weather. The WhiskerMic was a wire-thin microphone disguised among his whiskers. It recorded everything within a two-metre radius. If Kip and Finbar needed to check back on any details of their mission afterwards, they had a permanent record.

Once their helmets were off, Kip and Finbar had a look around. High in Neron's sky was a tiny blue ball of light.

Neron's sun, Kip guessed. *It must be light years away. No wonder it's so cold and dark here.*

As his eyes adjusted to the dark, Kip

saw they'd landed on the edge of a city.

Neron's buildings were made of cubes stacked on top of each other. They looked like massive kids' building blocks with flat panels on top.

Kip recognised them immediately. *Spinifex wind panels!* he thought. They had been invented by the aliens from the windy planet Spinifex, and were the most efficient wind-energy tech available. Kip knew they were incredibly expensive.

Suddenly Kip was struck by how quiet Neron seemed. He could see a spaceport in the distance, but it looked deserted.

Guess those rumours about Neron being a busy trading planet were wrong, he thought.

But then, how can they afford Spinifex wind panels?

Kip was about to mention this to Finbar when his 2iC yelped. The ground underneath their feet was moving! Was it an earth tremor? A deadly quake?

Finbar toppled over, landing on his furry backside.

'Are you okay?' Kip said. But Finbar didn't answer. With his excellent wolf vision, he'd spotted what was making the ground move.

They were standing on a giant rotating disc! A shallow, curved groove in the dirt stretched into the distance in both directions. The entire alien city was slowly

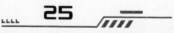

turning. At the same time, Kip felt the wind change direction.

The city must be turning to catch the most wind! Kip thought. He knew that the Spinifex wind panels could turn. But an entire rotating city would cost a bomb!

Suddenly, there was a shrill cry.

An alien had sneaked up behind them! And he had a group of friends with him.

The aliens were tall and rubbery. They had huge flapping ears and long, fleshy snouts with deep black nostrils. Their eyes were tiny black dots.

Kip knew that animals that lived in darkness underground on Earth were often almost totally blind. He guessed

these aliens wouldn't have much need for sight on such a dark planet. Maybe their other features were bigger than normal to make up for it.

Also, Kip couldn't help noticing the aliens were covered with deep scars. *They look like something out of a horror movie like 'Awful Aliens Attack IV'!*

The group of aliens came closer and closer. Then the lead alien shrieked something right in Kip's ear. It was so close, Kip could feel his icy spit through the heated balaclava.

EEEEEEEEEEEH!

CHAPTER 4

Startled, Kip quickly flicked his SpaceCuff to Translate mode.

TRANSLATE MODE

Greetings travellers.
You are very, very welcome.

Translate Mode

Kip nearly laughed in relief. Shrieking was this alien's way of being polite!

But when Kip looked into the alien's grinning face, he couldn't quite shake the feeling that the smile didn't reach his tiny eyes.

Still, Kip's Space Scout training had taught him to keep an open mind about all aliens. It was important to be polite until he knew more about them.

The lead alien shook Kip's hand energetically. His fingers felt like sloppy seaweed! But they still had a firm grip.

The alien grinned wider, just a bit too hard. He reminded Kip of dodgy spacecraft salespeople back on Earth.

Stop being so suspicious, Kip! he thought sternly. *They're perfectly friendly.*

'We're from planet Earth,' Kip said. His SpaceCuff started screeching, translating his speech into the Neron alien's language.

'Brilliant! Love the place,' the alien shrieked, grinning again.

But he knows nothing about us, Kip thought warily. *There's been no contact between Earth and Neron!*

'My people would like to know if you'd be willing to share some of your planet with us,' Kip said.

'That sounds like a very interesting proposal,' grinned the lead alien. 'For the right price, of course.'

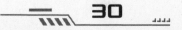

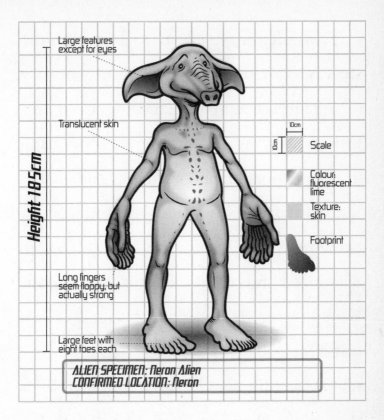

Large features
except for eyes

Translucent skin

Height 185cm

10cm

10cm

Scale

Colour:
fluorescent
lime

Texture:
skin

Footprint

Long fingers
seem floppy, but
actually strong

Large feet with
eight toes each

ALIEN SPECIMEN: Neron Alien
CONFIRMED LOCATION: Neron

WorldCorp had been right about the
aliens being smart businesspeople, then.
Fair enough, thought Kip. *There's no law
against it.*

Still, the more time Kip spent with the smooth-talking aliens, the more uneasy he felt. He couldn't put his finger on why, though.

Kip glanced at Finbar. Was his 2iC getting the same bad feeling? Kip guessed he was, because Finbar was nervously smoothing his fur. Clumps of it swept through the air.

A cluster floated past the lead alien's nose. He paused. There was a strange look on his face, like an idea was coming to him.

Then, out of nowhere, the alien made a horrible sound. It sounded like someone choking on a sock.

The alien's tiny eyes watered and bulged. His ears twitched wildly. Shallow,

rasping breaths escaped from its mouth. The alien dropped to his knees, clutching his throat with spidery hands.

'Is…is that some kind of local custom?' Finbar said to Kip uncertainly.

Kip shook his head. 'Can't be! Look at how the other aliens are crowding around.'

For a moment, they seemed as confused as Kip and Finbar. Then the lead alien moaned something too low for the SpaceCuff to register. A moment later, all the aliens suddenly fell to the ground, clutching at their throats too.

Finbar looked stricken, but something about it all reminded Kip of the last time he'd faked being sick, so his mum would

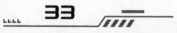

let him stay home from school.

But it was too risky to just ignore the aliens. They could be dying! Although Kip had a feeling that they weren't trustworthy, it was just a hunch. And his Space Scout training taught him never to leave an alien in distress. He had to help!

Down on his knees, Kip held a finger under the lead alien's snout. He didn't seem to be breathing.

Kip's heart began to pound. This was obviously serious! He couldn't believe he'd suspected the aliens of faking only seconds ago.

He could be holding his breath, niggled the voice in Kip's head.

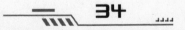

But Kip shoved his doubts aside firmly. Right now, he needed to focus on helping the aliens.

Kip rummaged in his backpack for his first aid kit. He needed his LifeBubble urgently.

Kip could simply breathe into the mouthpiece of the LifeBubble. An edible oxygen-filled bubble would pop into the alien's mouth, filling it with air. It was quick and hygienic. Except…

I've left my first aid kit on board MoNa, Kip realised. *I'll have to give mouth-to-mouth the old-fashioned way!*

Human mouth-to-mouth was gross enough. It would be even worse on Neron's

aliens, with their rubbery lips and long, soft noses.

Kip shuddered. He leant down to plant his mouth on the lead alien's.

Then the alien suddenly snapped his eyes open. 'Help us,' he wheezed. 'We're terribly allergic to something…'

He rolled his tiny eyes at Finbar. Then the alien collapsed in a loud coughing fit.

Kip's mind raced. The air was full of Finbar's fur. What if *that* was what the aliens were allergic to?

'What can we do?' Finbar asked anxiously. He hated to see anyone in pain.

'Your Earthling first aid won't help,' the alien said quickly. For a moment, his voice

sounded normal. 'Ancient Neron lore tells of a berry that grows on a thorny water plant. It cures all ills.' The alien paused, gasping again. 'It's our only hope.'

'Where do we find this plant?' Kip asked urgently.

'The lake district,' the alien croaked, trembling. Then, with a final wheeze, he fainted dramatically.

Finbar gasped. 'We've got to find the lake district. Immediately!'

CHAPTER 5

Finbar turned to Kip, his eyes enormous and sad. He put his paws under his chin in a begging pose.

Kip could tell that Finbar felt guilty. After all, it was his fur that seemed to be making the aliens sick.

Even if he didn't quite trust the aliens,

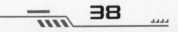

Kip couldn't say no to Finbar. Besides, finding the plant would be a good way of exploring the planet. And maybe he'd get to the bottom of the aliens' suspicious behaviour as well.

'Let's find that plant,' Kip said shortly.

He thought he saw a flicker of a triumphant smile on the passed-out alien's face. But then it was gone.

Finbar's ears twitched in relief. 'We'll get to the Lake District faster if we use our E-Zee-Flights.'

Nodding, Kip unzipped the front pocket of his backpack. At once, WorldCorp's newest gadget popped out.

E-Zee-Flights were light but strong

carbon-steel chopper blades. The blades were stored inside the front pocket of Kip's and Finbar's backpacks. Powerful mini engines and fuel cells were built into the base of the packs.

Putting his backpack on, Kip yanked the ripcord dangling from the bottom. The blades jumped into life. Kip lifted smoothly off his feet and tipped forward. Finbar activated his E-Zee-Flight and lifted off too.

Kip turned to Finbar. He knew that Finbar's nose was so skilled, it could detect changes in the air's moisture levels. The air would get wetter the closer they got to the lake district.

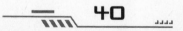

Can fly at altitudes of up to 1000 metres

E-ZEE-FLIGHT

Regular backpack as well as a personal flight device

Activation ripcord behind panel

'My nose says it's this way,' said Finbar, sniffing the air carefully.

With Finbar's nose leading the way, they quickly left the gleaming cube city behind.

Under their feet, Kip could just make out small ponds, their banks bare and dusty. *If any water plants ever grew there,* he thought, *they haven't been there for a long time.*

The further they flew, the more nervous Kip became. A strong wind had whipped up, and it was getting harder to stay on course.

'There!' Finbar yelled, pointing. A huge black lake spread out beneath them.

Kip tried to steer his E-Zee-Flight down to the bank of the lake, but the winds were practically cyclone-strength by now.

Kip's chopper blades were no match for the full force of Neron's winds. They

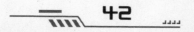

groaned dangerously as they tried to spin against the wind.

I've got a bad feeling about —
RIIIIIP!

'*Aaaargh!*' Kip screamed. With a sickening wrench, his blades tore off and spun away into the darkness. He was plunging towards the black lake, face-first!

Kip hurtled towards the surface, bracing himself for the icy water.
SPROOOOIING!

It should have been the bomb of the twenty-fourth century. But there was no splash at all. Even weirder, Kip didn't sink beneath the water.

He bounced off the surface!

Instead of water, the alien lake was filled with black, rubbery goo. *It's like bouncing on a custard trampoline!* Kip thought, relieved and thrilled at the same time. *Not that I've ever actually done that…*

Kip jumped quickly up and down. 'This stuff is awesome!' he yelled.

He waved at Finbar to come in. Finbar had managed to steer his E-Zee-Flight down to the dry ground at the edge of the lake. He walked slowly into the water to meet Kip. Almost immediately, he began to sink beneath the goo.

GLOP GLOP GLOP

It sounded like boiling mud.

'Keep moving!' Kip called to Finbar.

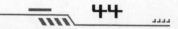

He'd quickly discovered that when he was running or jumping fast, he could move across the lake's surface. But if he slowed down for even a second, he sank.

Finbar kicked his legs wildly. Panting, he managed to pull himself back up to the surface. He started bouncing madly.

'Check out my double backward somersault with a twisting half pike!' Kip whooped. He sprang into the air and pulled off the trick perfectly.

'I wish Alien Lake Bouncing was an official sport in the Interplanetary Games,' Kip called, spinning in mid-air.

But Finbar was busy scanning for anything that looked like the miracle plant.

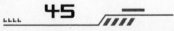

His wolfish eyesight was sharp, even in the gloom.

'There's nothing growing here,' Finbar said after a good look around. He and Kip were jogging across the lake side-by-side.

Kip saw Finbar was right. The lake's banks were eroded. There were rough holes where it looked like plants had been pulled out, and twigs and squashed berries littered the ground. But any living plants were long gone.

'Why would they need so much of the miracle cure?' Kip wondered aloud, his suspicions about the aliens returning.

Finbar shrugged. He was too soft-hearted to be suspicious.

Those aliens can't have deadly allergies every day, Kip thought to himself. *So maybe they're using this 'miracle cure' for something else...*

CHAPTER 6

'Check out that big rock!' Finbar called, interrupting Kip's thoughts. 'There's something growing on it.'

Kip bent his knees and launched himself into the air. With one almighty bounce, he landed next to the rock Finbar was pointing at.

Sticking out from a hole in the rock was

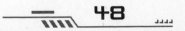

a big, ugly plant with sharp thorns on the woody stem. Unlike Earth's green plants, this one was completely white, since it grew in the dark. Thick purple goo oozed around the stem.

Kip squinted closer. He saw lots of milky-white berries clustered all over the plant. They had to be the ones the aliens had described.

Kip just needed to pick the berries. Then they could get back to the aliens and cure them. *Or find out what's really going on,* Kip added silently.

Kip bounced once and launched himself onto the rock to pick the berries.

Feels kinda warm and squishy for a rock…

NNNNNNNNNAAA ARRRRGH!

There was a horrible, gut-churning roar, and Kip was thrown into the air.

'*Whoa!*' he yelled as he landed on the rubbery water.

He was almost paralysed with shock! It took him a second to realise there wasn't a *rock* in the middle of the rubbery lake. It was actually the tip of *something's nose*. And that something was...

'A lake beast!' shrieked Finbar.

'Stay back!' Kip called to Finbar, who was bouncing over to help. If Kip was

injured, he wanted Finbar in one piece to rescue him.

Kip was furious. The aliens hadn't mentioned that a horrible, raging beast lived in the lake.

Now Kip knew for sure the aliens weren't to be trusted. He still didn't know why they wanted the plant, or whether they really were sick. But a decent alien would have mentioned this monstrous beast!

Again the creature roared, louder than twenty asteroids colliding.

It bared its rotten brown fangs at Kip. The beast was huge, with cruel eyes, leathery skin and spikes down its back like a dinosaur.

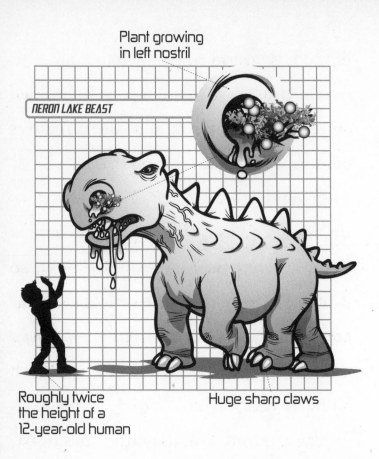

Plant growing
in left nostril

NERON LAKE BEAST

Roughly twice
the height of a
12-year-old human

Huge sharp claws

I'd be angry too, if I looked like that,
Kip thought.

'Duck!' yelled Finbar as the beast
swiped its claws at Kip. He bounced out

of the way just in time.

The beast gave a chilling cry. It thrashed around looking for Kip, sending tidal waves of rubbery water across the lake.

It can't see me properly, Kip guessed, as the beast's claws whistled past his ear.

The beast lived in near darkness, so it probably had terrible eyesight. *Still, its hearing and sense of smell probably make up for that,* thought Kip. He knew it would catch him eventually.

The more Kip dodged the lake beast, the angrier it got. Its beady eyes rolled back in its head. Drool dripped from its fangs.

'RUN!' Finbar yelled.

Kip shook his head. The aliens had sent him here for that plant, surely knowing about the lake beast. They must want that plant badly.

If he got it, Kip knew he'd have power over them. That could be useful in finding out what the devious Neron aliens were up to.

The beast lunged towards him. Kip gasped, exhausted. As well as dodging the beast, he still had to move fast enough to keep from sinking into the gloop.

I can't take this much longer, he thought.

Mentally, he ran through the contents of his backpack. There had to be something in there that could help!

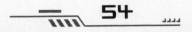

Ration pack with retractable toothpicks... useless right now.

Finbar's fur clippers... why had he brought those?

Then...

Of course! My Sooth-a-Torch! Why hadn't he thought of it before?

The Sooth-a-Torch had been developed for the first ever mission to the planet Sookilala, where the aliens looked like giant, constantly crying babies.

It shot out a beam of light like any normal torch. But the light-waves were at a special soothing frequency, and the torch also played a lullaby that tamed even the most restless aliens.

Kip wrenched his backpack open and grabbed the torch from inside.

Let's hope it works on lake beasts too! he thought.

CHAPTER 7

The rubbery surface of the lake rocked violently. The beast lumbered towards Kip, sniffing him out with its gaping nostrils. Globs of purple snot rained down everywhere.

But this time, Kip stayed put. He bounced on the spot, just enough to keep from sinking.

'Move, Kip!' yelled Finbar. 'It's almost on top of you!'

Closer and closer the beast came. Kip felt its warm, stinky breath on his skin. The beast raised its claws, and…

With one swift move, Kip engaged his Sooth-a-Torch.

A soft beam of light hit the lake beast's eyes and a gentle tune filled the air. Kip felt his own hammering heart slow down a few beats.

The lake beast blinked.

It stopped roaring.

Its gaping mouth seemed to smile. And in the back of its throat, the lake beast made a sweet cooing sound.

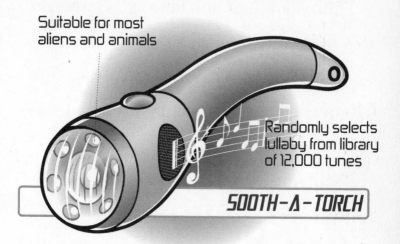

Suitable for most
aliens and animals

Randomly selects
lullaby from library
of 12,000 tunes

SOOTH-A-TORCH

The Sooth-a-Torch had worked perfectly!

The lake beast blinked and cocked its head at Kip. *Aw, it's kinda cute,* he thought. *As far as hideous monsters go.*

Obviously, Finbar thought the same thing. Kip's 2iC was already digging in his backpack for treats to feed the beast.

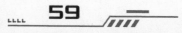

Finbar held out a paw to it. 'Try these chips,' he said kindly. 'They're Flamin' Asteroid flavour. My *flavourite*.'

Kip tried not to laugh. Finbar was such a softie!

'You're not so bad, are you, boy?' Finbar added. 'You just needed someone to treat you nicely.'

Finbar's words stuck in Kip's head.

Of course! he thought. *If the aliens wanted those berries so badly, they probably did all kinds of cruel things to the lake beast to get them.* No wonder it was suspicious of everyone who came to its lake.

Now that Kip and Finbar had shown the beast some kindness, it seemed to be

eating out of their hands. Literally!

The beast waded through the rubbery lake towards Finbar. It was too heavy to bounce across the surface like Kip and Finbar.

With a soft snuffle, the beast sucked up the chips in Finbar's paw. When all the chips were gone, the beast nuzzled its purple snotty snout into the crook of Finbar's arm.

'Can we harvest those berries now, eh, boy?' said Finbar, offering the beast more chips.

Happily munching, the beast didn't seem to mind Finbar and Kip plucking the berries from the plant in its nose.

Kip stored them safely in the side pocket of his backpack and zipped it closed. Finbar went on stroking the beast's nose.

Kip was determined to find out exactly what the aliens were up to. Why were they really so desperate to get their hands on the berries? Something told him that whatever the reason, it wouldn't be good.

No way am I letting the aliens get away with something dodgy! he thought firmly.

There was just one problem. Kip had crashed his E-Zee-Flight when they arrived at the lake. Finbar's wasn't strong enough to carry both of them.

After all that bouncing around, walking all the way back to the city wouldn't be

much fun. *Unless,* Kip thought suddenly, *the beast wouldn't mind doing his new best friends a favour?*

'Do you think the lake beast is amphibious?' Kip asked Finbar.

Finbar nodded. 'Possibly. A lot of Earth's reptiles are.' He paused. 'Kip, you're not thinking…'

But Kip had already bounced over to the lake beast. After a friendly pat on the beast's slimy chest, Kip hauled himself up onto its back.

'Giddy up!' Kip yelled, offering Finbar a hand up. The beast seemed to like having passengers.

'Take us to the city, boy,' Finbar said.

He guided the beast by throwing Flamin'
Asteroid chips on the ground.

The beast began to trot, and then picked
up pace. It was heavy, so every step was
bone-rattling. Its gigantic feet sprayed dust
as it galloped across the eroded ponds on
the way back to the city.

'Wooooo-hoooo!' Kip shouted, holding
on tight. He hardly even noticed how slimy
it was to ride an alien lake beast bareback.

He couldn't wait to tell Jett when he
got home!

CHAPTER 8

When the beast arrived in the cube city, there was no sign of the aliens.

'Hello?' Kip yelled up at the nearby gleaming towers.

'We've found the miracle cure!' Kip yelled. He waved the backpack full of berries in the air.

'Good job, Earthling,' screeched a

chillingly familiar voice. It was the lead alien, alone this time. And he looked to be in tip-top health.

The lake beast gave a horrible grunt. Its beady eyes rolled in its head. With one almighty move, it bucked Kip and Finbar from its back. It thundered away, roaring in terror.

Kip landed with a thump on the ground. *Poor lake beast!* he thought. *Looks like I was right about the aliens treating him badly. He's terrified of them!*

Kip and Finbar picked themselves up.

'I see you met Tiny,' the alien smirked.

'Why didn't you warn us about him?' Kip snapped.

'Oh, Tiny's normally so friendly,' the alien chuckled. 'We didn't think you'd have any problems getting the berries from him.'

Kip rolled his eyes. It was obvious the alien was lying. It seemed there was no point in asking the aliens directly what they were up to. Kip would have to be cleverer.

Casually, he unzipped his backpack. 'It's great to see you're feeling so much better,' he said to the aliens. 'I guess you won't be needing this anymore.'

He tilted the bag, as if to pour the berries out.

At once, the alien coughed loudly. 'Oh, no. We still need the miracle cure,' he said quickly. 'Our illness comes and goes.'

'Still, it doesn't sound life-threatening,' Kip continued, pretending to tip the bag even further.

Suddenly, the alien tried to snatch the bag from Kip's hand. But Kip was quick to pull it out of reach.

He could tell he was driving the alien crazy.

Suddenly, the alien snapped and began screeching furiously. 'You'll never be able to sell the berries, greedy Earthling. You don't know the right people!'

Ah-ha! Kip thought, as the alien ranted. *The aliens must be trading these berries illegally!*

He quickly whispered his theory to

Finbar, still holding the bag out of reach of the Neron alien.

Finbar nodded gravely.

'WorldCorp heard rumours Neron was a trading planet,' he whispered back. 'The spaceport looked deserted when we landed. But if the trade's illegal, that makes sense. Everything would be hush-hush.'

Everything Finbar said supported Kip's theory. Now Kip needed to prove it.

'I'm surprised you're allowed to harvest those plants at all,' Kip said to the aliens.

The waterways of Neron were eroded. It looked as if the Neron aliens had been pulling the whole berry plant out of the ground, rather than just picking the

berries. Harvesting the berries this way was clearly an environmental disaster. There were tough intergalactic laws protecting planets' ecosystems. Kip knew all about them because of Earth's own problems.

The lead alien laughed scornfully, making Kip's skin crawl.

'We're *not* allowed. That's why the berries are so valuable.'

Kip and Finbar swapped glances.

'Demand for the berries is unstoppable,' the alien screeched.

'But the plant only grows when fertilised by the lake beast's snot.

It's winter at the moment, though, and the beast is hibernating in the big lake.'

Kip shuddered. *Eww!*

'In summer, the beast leaves snot in the smaller ponds around Neron. We harvested the plants growing there ages ago,' said the alien.

'And there was one last plant growing in the beast's nostril,' Kip finished.

Finbar nodded with a smile on his whiskery face. 'How interesting,' he said encouragingly. 'Go on.'

Kip glared at Finbar. Why was he being nice to the aliens now?

'The other aliens in our dark galaxy believe that eating the berries improves their eyesight. It's a load of space junk, of course. But the aliens pay heaps for them.'

The alien rubbed his spidery hands together greedily.

Environmental vandalism. An illegal trade in a fake medicine. That's what made the aliens rich, Kip thought, thinking of Neron's Spinifex wind panels.

The Intergalactic Enforcerbots would be *very* interested to hear about this!

CHAPTER 9

The Intergalactic Enforcerbots were space police, made up of custom-built all-terrain robots.

But before the Enforcerbots can charge the aliens, Kip thought desperately, *we have to prove what's going on here. Otherwise it's our word against theirs!*

Then Kip heard a surprising sound coming from Finbar's direction. It was a hideous screech!

For a second, Kip couldn't work out how or why Finbar was speaking the aliens' language. He checked his SpaceCuff for the translation.

TRANSLATE MODE

It's a load of old space junk, of course. But the aliens pay heaps for them.

Translate Mode

Of course. Finbar's WhiskerMic! It had secretly recorded everything the alien said. Finbar was simply playing it back.

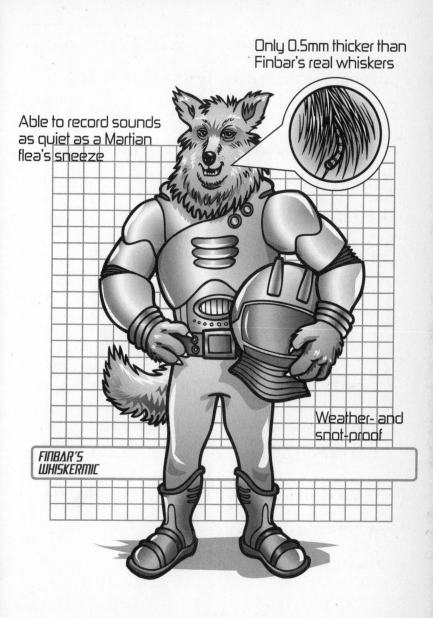

Only 0.5mm thicker than Finbar's real whiskers

Able to record sounds as quiet as a Martian flea's sneeze

Weather- and snot-proof

FINBAR'S WHISKERMIC

75

'Ha!' said Kip to the alien. 'We've got proof you're breaking all kinds of inter-galactic laws.'

The lead alien laughed nastily. Then he screeched. A group of his friends appeared from inside a building.

At once, the aliens lunged at Finbar.

Heads down, Kip and Finbar sprinted away from them. As Kip ran, he called MoNa on his SpaceCuff.

'Send two Scramblers ASAP!' he panted, glancing over his shoulder. The aliens were right behind them.

They'd done so much running already on this mission! Kip's spaceboots felt like concrete.

Plus, running through the unfamiliar alien city was difficult in the dark.

Then suddenly, the entire city began to rotate under Kip's and Finbar's feet! Once again, it was turning to match the changing direction of the wind.

Kip stumbled. His feet scrabbled, trying to get a foothold on the shifting ground.

The lead alien loomed up behind him in the dark.

'Come on, MoNa!' Kip yelled at the sky. 'What's taking so –'

Then suddenly, the entire city lit up. It was like two bolts of lightning had struck at once.

At last! A pair of Scramblers beamed

down from MoNa high up in Neron's atmosphere.

Kip ran towards them, shielding his eyes. After being in the dark for most of the mission, the bright light stung his eyes badly.

Kip leapt into his Scrambler Beam. Finbar tried to do the same. But before he could make it safely, the lead alien reached out and grabbed at Finbar's whiskers.

'FIN!' Kip screamed.

If the aliens snatched his WhiskerMic, the evidence against them would be lost.

But then Kip's world began to scramble in front of him. His particles were being mixed up and beamed through space. Kip

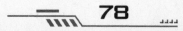

could do nothing to help Finbar now…

Seconds later, Kip found himself alone on the floor of MoNa's landing bay. His particles had reassembled perfectly, but he was frantic. What had happened to Finbar?

Kip paced up and down the bay. Without his 2iC, it was eerily quiet. The seconds dragged by. And then –

'What's up, Kip?' said a voice behind him.

Kip swung around. It was Finbar!

'You made it!' Kip yelled, giving Finbar a bear hug.

Or would that be a wolf hug? he thought, relieved.

Finbar looked like his normal self,

except he was missing all his whiskers on the right side.

'The aliens ripped them out,' Finbar said, rubbing his cheek. 'Those floppy fingers are surprisingly powerful.'

Kip winced. He didn't have whiskers, but he imagined pulling them out would really hurt!

'I managed to get free, though,' Finbar finished.

'And the recording?' Kip asked nervously.

Finbar chuckled. 'Luckily I keep the WhiskerMic on the left,' he said, pulling out a whisker that was a tiny bit thicker than the rest.

Finbar filled Kip in on every detail as they headed to the Bridge. When they got there, Kip flopped into his captain's chair. He couldn't wait to tell the Intergalactic Enforcerbots about Neron's aliens.

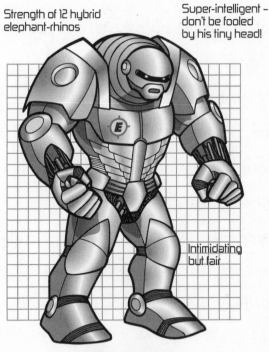

Strength of 12 hybrid elephant-rhinos

Super-intelligent – don't be fooled by his tiny head!

Intimidating but fair

Enforcerbot

Kip punched the number for the Enforcerbot command centre into his SpaceCuff.

An Enforcerbot answered on the first ring. His picture shot up on Kip's screen. His eyes flashed red and blue as Kip told him all about the illegal activity on Neron.

'We wondered how that planet got so rich,' the Enforcerbot said. 'The answer was trading in illegal substances and, from the sound of it, environmental vandalism.'

Satisfied, Kip hung up.

His mission was complete…almost.

CHAPTER 10

'No relaxing yet,' chimed MoNa. 'You've got a mission report to write.'

It was a WorldCorp rule that Space Scouts had to file a report as soon as they'd completed a mission. MoNa loved rules, and she made sure Kip stuck to every one.

Turning to the holographic console, Kip scrolled to the screen he needed.

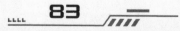

CAPTAIN'S LOG
Neron

....

Conditions: A cold, dark planet unsuitable for humans. Trampoline water was fun, though.

Locals: The aliens are wealthy, clever businesspeople. It's a pity their only trade is illegal.

Appearance: There's no way to put this politely. The aliens are ugly enough to curdle Martian yak milk.

Fauna: A single vicious lake beast was the only example spotted. Luckily!

Recommendation: Neron is not Earth 2. Trust me – you don't want to go there and check.

KIP KIRBY, SPACE SCOUT #50

Kip shivered. Even thinking about Neron's dark atmosphere was enough to make him feel cold and gloomy.

Luckily, WorldCorp had recently installed a MoodBeach aboard MoNa.

After long flights, Space Scouts tended to feel a bit cooped up. Being inside all the time, away from natural light, was known to put humans in a bad mood. The MoodBeach was WorldCorp's solution.

Kip and Finbar headed for MoNa's top deck, where the new MoodBeach was located.

A circular door slid open, revealing a perfectly blank white room beyond.

Finbar looked disappointed. MoNa was

one of the newest starships in WorldCorp's fleet. Normally her gadgets were the coolest available.

'Not much of a beach,' he grumbled, his remaining whiskers drooping.

'Not yet,' Kip grinned, grabbing a touch-screen remote from the wall.

Using the controller, Kip could customise the indoor beach just the way he wanted it. For the sky, he chose 91% blue with 9% puffy white clouds. Immediately, Kip's perfect sky popped up on the ceiling.

Then he set the temperature to 'Tropical Island at Midday'. When he twiddled the bird control, the sound of gulls filled the room.

Controls change
weather, temperature,
colour scheme and more

Virtual volleyball
available

MoNa 4000 MoodBeach

WORLDCORP

Beach-themed snacks
in MoNa's kitchen for
full beach experience

'Gulls? Booor-ing!' laughed Finbar.
'How about Martian Macaws instead?'

Kip changed the bird setting so the
indoor beach was flooded with macaws
singing.

When Kip adjusted the sand and water controls, the floor slid away to reveal fine white sand and turquoise water. There was just the number of gentle, lapping waves Kip had requested.

Finally, Kip played with the sunlight controller. He knew that back in the 2000s, people used to go to the beach to get suntans.

Can't believe anyone did anything so dangerous! Kip thought to himself. In the year 2354, it was impossible to go outside without Factor 10,000 sunscreen all over your body.

Anyway, Brilliantans are so much cooler than ordinary suntans, Kip decided.

Brilliantans were one of WorldCorp's weirder inventions. They allowed indoor beach users to select what colour they'd like their skin to turn.

All colours were available – blue, pink, orange and even a sickly shade of green. Special light rays reacted with a pigment in human skin, turning your body a different colour all over.

'Think I'll go blue,' Kip said. His mum wouldn't be too impressed, but oh well. Good thing Brilliantans were only temporary!

Kip yanked off his spacesuit. Underneath, he had on the T-shirt he'd worn to the One Moon Shopping Mall. It seemed

like light years ago he'd been checking out the micro-rhinos with Jett!

Kip settled back on the sand. Almost at once, he felt warm, happy and relaxed. The MoodBeach was definitely working. Plus, Kip's skin was already a light shade of blue.

He'd make quite a splash next time he went virtu-surfing!

THE END